WISDOM
of
KITTENS

Compiled by
Franchesca Ho Sang

HYLAS

HYLAS

Hylas Publishing®
129 Main Street, Ste. C
Irvington, NY 10533
www.hylaspublishing.com

Hylas Publishing
Publisher: Sean Moore
Publishing Director: Karen Prince
Art Director: Gus Yoo
Designer: La Tricia Watford
Editor: Franchesca Ho Sang
Proofreader: Emily G.F. Beekman

ISBN:1–59258–254–4
ISBN 13/EAN: 978-1592-58252-5

Library of Congress Cataloging–in–Publication Data available upon request.
Printed and bound in Singapore
Distributed in the United States by Publishers Group West
Distributed in Canada by Publishers Group Canada
First American Edition published in 2006

2 4 6 8 10 9 7 5 3 1

WISDOM

of

KITTENS

Compiled by
Franchesca Ho Sang

www.hylaspublishing.com

"The superior man thinks always of virtue; the **common** man thinks of **comfort**."

–*Confucius*

"To accomplish **great things**, we must not only act, but also **dream**; not only plan, but also believe."

–*Anatole France*

"Expect the best, plan for the worst, and prepare to be surprised."

–Denis Waitley

"An eye for
an eye only
ends up
making the
whole world
blind."

–Ghandi

"It is a **rough road**
that **leads to** the heights of **greatness**."

–Frank Borman

"There is no feeling
more comforting

than knowing
you are right next to
the one you love."

–*Anonymous*

"Stand up
to your obstacles
and do something
about them."

–*Norman Vincent Peale*

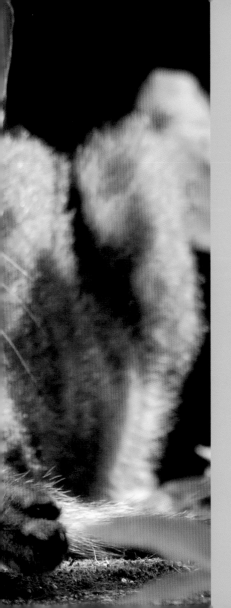

"The **best** thing
to spend on
your children is
your **time**."

–*Louise Hart*

"'Tis the part of a **wise man** to keep himself today for tomorrow, and not venture all his eggs in one basket."

–Miguel de Cervantes Saavedra

"Cats are connoisseurs of comfort."

–James Herriot

"**Faith** is by which a shattered world shall **emerge** into the **light**."

–*Helen Keller*

"**Life** is a mirror and will **reflect** back to the **thinker** what he thinks into it."

–*Ernest Holmes*

"Even a cat is a lion
in her own lair."

–Indian proverb

"Life is like riding a bicycle.

To keep your balance
you must **keep moving**."

–*Albert Einstein*

"The desire for safety stands against every great and noble enterprise."

–*Tacitus*

"One of the greatest discoveries a man makes, one of his greatest surprises, is to find he can do what he was afraid he couldn't."

–Henry Ford

"Don't be afraid to **expand yourself,** to **step out** of your comfort zone. That's where the joy and **adventure lie**."

–Herbie Hancock

"Concentration and mental toughness are the margins of victory."

–Bill Russell

"The only way to **find** the **limits** of the possible is by **going beyond** them into the impossible."

–Arthur C. Clarke

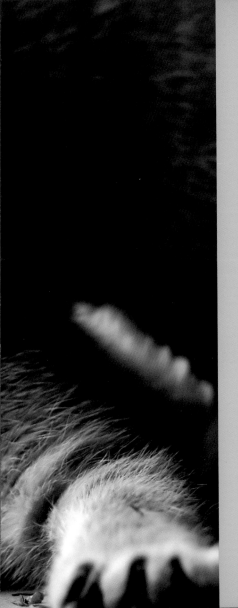

"In every
real man a
child is
hidden that
wants to **play**."

–*Friedrich Nietzsche*

"The **smallest** feline is a **masterpiece**."

–Leonardo da Vinci

"We must accept finite disappointment, but **never lose** infinite **hope**."

–*Martin Luther King, Jr.*

"Jump. It is not as wide as you think."

–Joseph Campbell

"Self-confidence is the **first** requisite to great **undertakings**."

–*Samuel Johnson*

"It's not our differences
that divide us

it is our inability to recognize, accept, and **celebrate** those **differences**."

–*Audre Lorde*

"Live and **work** but do not forget to **play**,

to have fun in life and really **enjoy** it."

–*Eileen Caddy*

"Only those who **attempt** the absurd...
will achieve the **impossible**."

–M.C. Escher

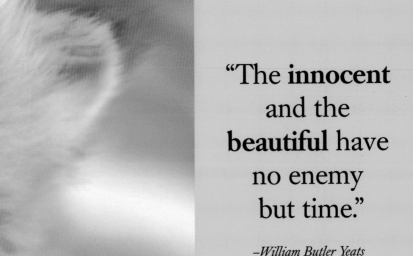

"The **innocent** and the **beautiful** have no enemy but time."

–William Butler Yeats

"The secret to creativity is **knowing** how to hide your **success**."

–*Albert Einstein*

"Love one another,
but make not a bond of love:

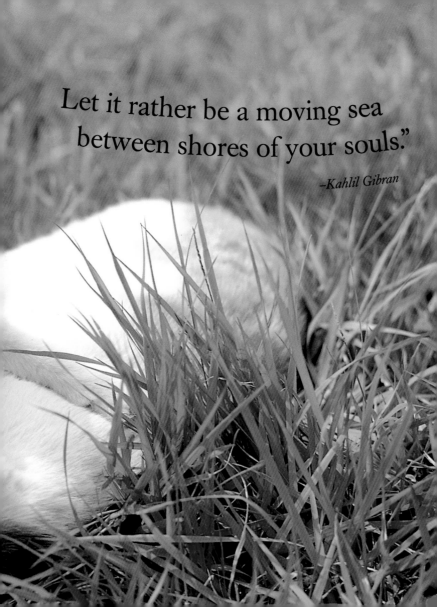

Let it rather be a moving sea
between shores of your souls."

–*Kahlil Gibran*

"**Lack** of loyalty is
one of the major causes of failure
in every walk of life."

–*Napoleon Hill*

"Don't be afraid
to go out
on a limb.
That's where
the fruit is."

–H. Jackson Browne

"Whatever you can do
        or dream you can begin it.
Boldness has genius,
        power and magic in it."

–Goethe

"Dreams are today's **answers** to tomorrow's questions."

–Edgar Cayce

"The whole world steps aside
for the man
who knows where he is going."

–*Anonymous*

"Who has never tasted what is bitter does not know what is sweet."

–*German proverb*

"First thoughts are the strongest."

–Allen Ginsberg

"Sadness is but a wall
between two gardens."

–Kahlil Gibran

"Self-assurance
is two thirds of success."

–Proverb

"Act as though you cannot fail but keep a humble spirit."

–Anonymous

"A friend may well be reckoned the **masterpiece** of nature."

–*Ralph Waldo Emerson*

"Courage doesn't always roar. Sometimes **courage is the quiet voice** at the end of the day saying. 'I will try again tomorrow.'"

–*Mary Anne Radmache*

"Friendship is the essential partnership."

–Aristotle

"Be who you are
and say what you feel,
because those who mind
don't matter, and those
who matter don't mind."

–Dr. Seuss

"Our **greatest** glory
is not in never falling,
but rising everytime we **fall**."

–*Confucius*

"If you can **dream** it, you can **do it**."
–*Walt Disney*

"In every woman there is a queen."

–Norwegian proverb

"The **future** belongs to those who prepare for it **today**."

–*Malcolm X*

"Wise men
ne'er sit and wail
their woes."

–William Shakespeare

"There are only two forces that **unite men**— fear and **interest**."

–*Napoleon Bonaparte*

"**We cannot** always
build the future
of our youth,
but we can **build**
our youth
for the **future**."

–*Franklin D. Roosevelt*

"Some men go through a forest and see no firewood."

–*English proverb*

"The price of **greatness** is responsibility."

–*Abraham Lincoln*

"Only the **unknown** frightens men."

–Antoine de Saint–Exupéry

"A **peaceful** man does more than a learned one."

–*Pope John XXIII*

"Hope is the **dream** of the soul **awake**."

–*French proverb*

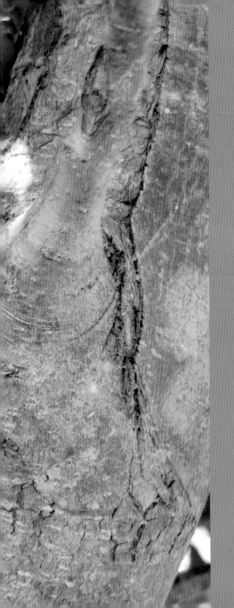

"My only advice is to stay aware, **listen carefully** and yell for help if you need it."

–*Judy Blume*

PICTURE CREDITS

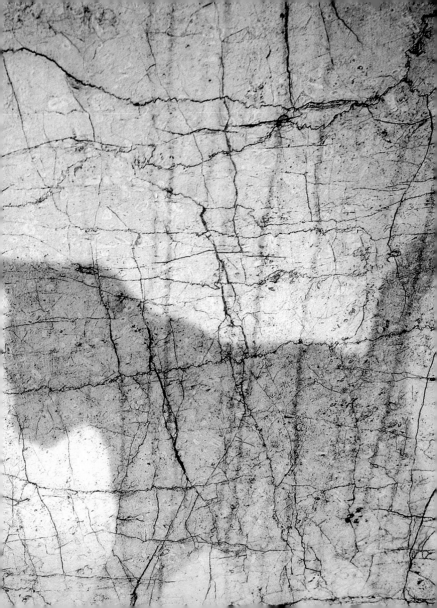